To Hildy, who has been known to deviate from
a recipe or two, but always cooks with love
—K.W.

For Pat and Ken,
with special thanks to Emma and Ann

—W.H.

Margaret K. McElderry Books
An imprint of Simon & Schuster Children's Publishing Division
1230 Avenue of the Americas, New York, New York 10020
Text copyright © 2007 by Karma Wilson
Illustrations copyright © 2007 by Will Hillenbrand
All rights reserved, including the right of reproduction in whole or in part in any form.
Book design by Ann Bobco and Sammy Yuen.
The text for this book is set in Blockhead.
The illustrations for this book are rendered in ink and egg tempera on canvas.
Manufactured in China
10 9 8 7 6 5 4 3 2 1
Library of Congress Cataloging-in-Publication Data
Wilson, Karma.
Whopper cake / by Karma Wilson.—1st ed.
p. cm.
Summary: Granddad bakes Grandma a whopper of a birthday cake. Includes recipe and directions for chocolate cake.
ISBN-13: 978-0-689-83844-6
ISBN-10: 0-689-83844-1
[1. Birthday cake—Fiction. 2. Tall tales. 3. Stories in rhyme.] I. Title.
PZ8.3W6976 Gr 2007
[E—dc21
00-058742

FIRST
EDITION

Whopper Cake

Karma Wilson

Will Hillenbrand

Margaret K. McElderry Books
New York London Toronto Sydney

Today is Grandma's birthday,
and Granddad has an itchin'
to bake a whopper chocolate cake
and traumatize the kitchen.

Grandma scolds, "Now listen up, don't make a fuss, you hear? Land sakes! I swear your cakes are getting bigger every year!"

While Grandma runs some errands,
Granddad ties his apron tight,
props the tattered cookbook up,
and sets to do things right.

(Right odd, that is . . .)

"Who thought up this recipe?
The cake will be too small.
If I can't make a WHOPPER cake,
I'll bake no cake at all!"

Granddad grabs a bowl and spoon,
and makes a frightful clatter.
Ingredients go flying
as he starts to mix the batter!

"I'm sure no cook," says Granddad,
"but it would seem to me,
two cups of sugar ain't enough.
I'll put in twenty-three."
(Twenty-three pounds, that is . . .)

Granddad cries, "This bowl won't do!"
and scratches at his head.
"Eureka, I have just the thing . . .

. . . we'll use the pickup bed!

Go start the old jalopy, boys!
and back it in real tight.
Grandma's gonna be surprised
when she gets home tonight!"

Recipe says four fresh eggs.
In go eighty-six.
Recipe says two cups flour.
Ten go in the mix.

(Ten bags, that is . . .)

"I need a bigger stirrin' stick!
This spoon is mighty poor.
Head down to the fishin' boat
and fetch me up an oar."

Granddad holds the paddle firm
and sets himself to mixin'.
"I'm thinking that old cookstove
might not hold this cake we're fixin'."

Recipe says one pinch salt.
Granddad "pinches" more.
Recipe says one cup cocoa.
In go twenty-four.

(Twenty-four boxes, that is . . .)

Granddad licks the mixin' oar.
"It tastes just like a dream."
But Grandma likes her birthday cake
topped off with fresh ice cream!

"Let's head down to the market, boys,
and buy up all they've got.
A treat so cold is pleasing
on a day so scorchin' hot!"

The drive to town is mighty warm,
this day in mid-July.
While that sun is blazin' down,
that cake is raisin' high!
(Ten feet high, that is . . .)

Drivin' home we're followed
by a chocolate-scented cloud.
And when folks get a whiff of it,
there gathers quite a crowd!

No one's ever seen a cake
so big and wide and tall.
Granddad cries, "Step right up,
there's plenty here for all!"

Everybody pitches in
to help us decorate.
With shovels we spread frosting,
then we settle down to wait.

(Wait to dig in, that is . . .)

We all hide till Grandma comes . . .

. . . and then we yell,

"SURPRISE!"

And when she sees that birthday cake,
she can't believe her eyes!

"All this fuss for me?" she asks.
"But why, for heaven's sake?"

"Your heart's so big," says Granddad,

"you deserve a

WHOPPER CAKE!"

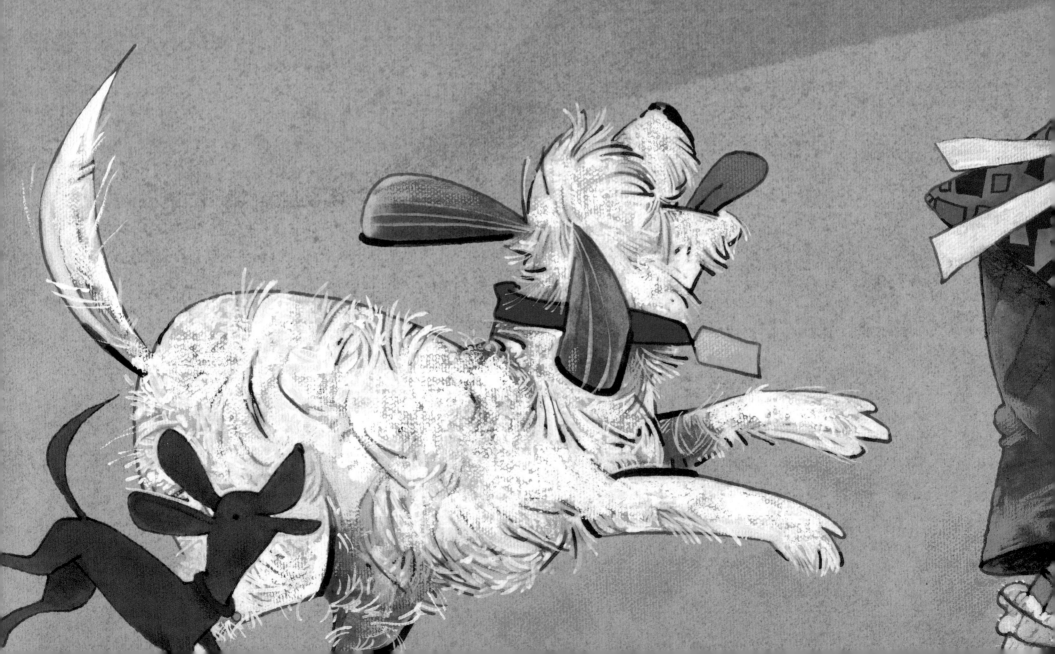

Grandma blows her candles out.

"I've just one wish, I guess.

I'll enjoy this whopper cake . . .

. . . and **YOU** clean up the mess."

(The WHOPPER MESS, that is . . .)

YOU CAN BAKE A WHOPPER CAKE!

Granddad says:

First ya need to gather the ingredients. Ask your favorite grown-up to help you rustle up the following:

1 cup unsweetened cocoa powder
1 cup butter + 1 tablespoon butter for greasin' the pan
1 cup very hot water
1 cup buttermilk
2 eggs
1 tablespoon vanilla extract or imitation vanilla extract
2-1/2 cups white sugar
3 cups cake flour + 1 tablespoon flour for flourin' the pan
1 teaspoon baking soda
1 teaspoon salt
1 teaspoon baking powder

Preheat the oven to 350° Fahrenheit. You'll need a pan. Don't fret none if ya don't have a pickup bed handy—a 9" x 13" cake pan works just as well and makes a nice, big whopper cake!

Make sure ya grease and flour the pan real good or the cake will stick to it like a bear's nose to honey!

Next, ya best get to mixin'. Pour the cocoa powder and butter in a big bowl with the hot water and stir it up real good until all the lumps and bumps are gone. Then add the buttermilk, eggs, and vanilla and keep on stirrin' until the batter's light and creamy. Sift in all the dry ingredients and whip it up real nice with one of them fancy electric mixers for two minutes. (Ya can use a stout wooden spoon if'n your arm is strong.) Pour that batter into yer pan and ask yer favorite grown-up to help

ya pop it in the oven. Be real careful-like 'cause that oven's hotter than a fritter in a fry pan!

Bake that cake fer about thirty minutes or until a knife inserted in the middle don't come out with a bunch of gook stickin' to it.

Let the cake cool for a half hour. Frost it with yer favorite chocolate or fudge frostin' and serve. It's best piled high with heaps of fresh vanilla ice cream! You can serve up sixteen people with this cake!

Oh, and Grandma says, "If'n ya know what's good fer ya, you'll help clean up the whopper mess!"